ROBO-RUNNERS

The Tin Man

www.damianharvey.co.uk

ARTS COUNCIL ENGLAND

Books in the **Robo-Runners** series:

ROBO-RUNNERS

The Tin Man

by DAMIAN HARVEY

Illustrated by Mark Oliver

Hodder Children's Books

A division of Hachette Children's Books

For Anne Finnis – for encouraging me to
write something longer

The door closed behind them with an airtight hiss. Crank turned and gave it a kick.

"Well thank you *very much*," he shouted. The door ignored him and the lock indicator turned from green to red.

There would be no going back. Crank was on his own.

Well … almost.

If Crank *had* been on his own it would have been easier. He could have made a run for it. He might even have had a chance to get away before the Tin Man arrived.

But Crank wasn't on his own. Al was there to help,

and before Crank could face the way they were
supposed to be going, Al started helping.

Crank found himself being pulled backwards
and dragged across the road towards the
collection zone. The ear-splitting screech of metal
on concrete filled the air as sparks flew up from
Crank's feet. His heels dug into the ground leaving
long grooves in the road like tramlines.

"Do you mind?" shouted Crank.

"Not at all," said Al, in his annoyingly polite
and helpful voice. "It is the least I can do."

"*No!*" shouted Crank. "The *least* you could do is let me go. The *least* you could do is give me a *chance* to get away from the Tin Man."

"Get away from the Tin Man?" said Al. "Why would you want to get away?"

"*Why?*" cried Crank, as Al dragged him on to the pavement at the other side of the road.

"Yes," said Al. "I thought *all* robots looked forward to the day they would be taken to the great recycling plant. Tired old robots go in and fresh new robots come out."

"Now let me think," said Crank, scratching at a piece of paint that was flaking off his head. "Why don't I want to have my wiring cut, my circuit boards ripped out, and my body melted down in a giant furnace so I can be turned into a toaster?"

"I am sure it is not like that," said Al. "Recycling is wonderful. Old useless robots go in, and bright new robots come out."

"But *I'm* still useful," shouted Crank.

"Of course you are," said Al, reassuringly. "All scrap metal is useful."

"*Scrap metal?*" cried Crank, "I'm not scrap metal. I'm a ZX TK 60 – top of the range, all-purpose, multifunction, home improvement robot. They don't make them like me any more, you know."

"You are right," said Al. "You are probably the very last one."

"The last one?" said Crank. "That means I must be worth *something* then."

"You are," said Al. "The money they got from selling you means your owners could afford the very latest in robot technology."

"Wow!" said Crank. "The *very* latest?"

"Yes," said Al, as he let go of Crank's arm. "The *very* latest ... Me."

Crank fell on to his back with a loud crunch.

"We have arrived at the collection zone," said Al.

Crank groaned. "I think you've dropped me on top of something," he said.

"Oh dear," said Al. "Let me help you."

"**NO!**" cried Crank. "I think you've *helped* enough, thank you very much."

Crank had landed on a small maintenance robot. It *had* looked a bit like a robotic crab, but now it looked rather flat.

"Oh dear," said Al, "you seem to have flattened it."

"Me!" cried Crank. "It wasn't *my* fault. *You* dropped me."

"Do not worry," said Al. "You are just feeling tired. Everything will be better once you have been recycled."

"But I don't want to be recycled!" cried Crank.

"There is nothing to worry about," said Al. "You will not be on your own. Look."

Crank looked. The collection zone was full of other robots. There were old street cleaner robots, domestic house robots, and engineering robots. There were robots of all shapes and sizes. There was even an old Fire and Rescue robot and a couple of crab-like maintenance robots – though one of them *did* look rather flat.

Apart from the second maintenance robot, which was desperately trying to keep away from Crank, the others were eagerly peering into the distance. It was as if they were waiting for something exciting to happen.

Then Crank realised … they were waiting for the Tin Man.

And they looked happy about it.

"They must be mad," said Crank.

"Not at all," said Al. "They are looking towards their future. This is a wonderful time for an old robot."

"Is it *really*?" said Crank. "*Well*, while they are busy looking to their future why don't I just run the other way?"

"I am sorry," said Al, "but I can not let you do that. I was told to bring you here for recycling. It would not be good if I failed in my first task."

"They won't thank you for it, you know," said Crank. "You'll work your joints right down to the washers and what will they do when you lose your ball bearings? They'll throw you on the scrap heap, that's what."

"When I am tired and worn out," said Al, "I will look forward to being recycled. You should look forward to it too. Old broken junk goes in and fresh new robots come out."

Crank opened his mouth to shout at Al, but the

sound was drowned out by the whine of engines as a Mark III robo-mule and transport trailer landed in the road.

The Tin Man had arrived.

The blast from the robo-mule's engines sent a
waste bin rolling across the street, scattering
rubbish as it clattered along.

The Tin Man sat high up in the driver's seat.
A wide-brimmed hat shaded his eyes and a scarf
hid the rest of his face from view. A long dark coat
hung to the top of his fancy boots where a pair of
spiked spurs glinted in the light.

The Tin Man took a silver bucket from beneath
his seat and stepped down on to the road. One
boot landed squarely on top of an empty can,
flattening it like a pancake. The Tin Man slid
the bucket beneath the robo-mule to catch drops

of oil as they dripped from a leaking valve, then he turned and kicked the squashed can.

Crank, Al and the other robots watched the can go spinning and clattering along the road. They all kept perfectly still, wondering what would happen next.

They didn't have long to wonder ...

In the collection zone one of the old street cleaning robots started to rattle and shake. The others shuffled away as the shaking and rattling got more frantic.

"Don't do it," said Crank. "Leave it alone!"

But the sight of the can lying there in the middle of the road, when it should have been in a waste bin, was just too much. Years of programming to keep the streets of Metrocity clean and litter-free got the better of the old robot.

The street cleaner made a sudden dash for the can. It *almost* got there too.

It was one step away from picking up the rubbish when the thunderous CRACK of an electro-whip split the air.

The whip coiled around the body of the old robot, crackling and spitting with electric charge. The coil pulled tight, pinning the robot's arms to its side.

"No one gets away from me," growled the Tin Man.

Blue sparks flickered across the surface of the robot, and wisps of smoke curled from its joints. Crank and the others watched in horror as the Tin Man dragged the robot towards him and picked it up. The Tin Man limped towards the back of the transport trailer and threw the old robot on to it like a pile of junk.

"Oh dear," said Al. "I think he should have waited with the rest of us."

Crank looked at Al in disbelief, but he and the other robots were watching the Tin Man as he re-coiled the electro-whip.

While everyone was busy looking the other way, Crank made up his mind. He'd noticed the Tin Man limping and felt sure that he wouldn't be able to run very fast. Crank knew that he *could* run fast … so that's what he did.

With the robo-mule and the other robots between them, Crank hoped the Tin Man wouldn't notice him running away from the collection zone.

Crank ran down an alleyway lined with doors. Rows of red indicator lights showed the doors were locked so Crank didn't waste time trying them. He knew that if he could just reach the corner and get out of sight he might have a chance to escape.

Crank ran as fast as he could, not daring to

look round in case the Tin Man had seen him and was already reaching for his electro-whip.

Only a few more steps and he'd be at the corner.

Four ... three ...

nearly there ...

two ...

A shout echoed down the alleyway ...

"Crank! Wait!"

It was Al.

Crank was halfway round the corner and into the next alleyway, but he stopped and peered back towards the collection zone. Al was bounding after him, waving his arms in the air. The other robots had gathered round the mouth of alleyway, eager to see what would happen.

"Where are you going?" shouted Al. "The Tin Man is here. It is time to go for recycling."

Crank couldn't believe it. Why couldn't Al just let him go ... and how did he manage to shout and still sound so annoyingly polite and helpful?

Crank was about to answer when a loud noise erupted from the collection zone. Robots tried frantically to get out of the way as something

came crashing between them. The robot at the front was sent flying as the thing finally broke through the crowd.

It was the Tin Man. He'd heard Al shouting and come to see what was going on.

For a moment everything went quiet as the Tin

Man stood there, silently watching.

Al stopped running and turned to face him.

"Oh! Hello, Mr Tin Man, sir," said Al. "We are sorry to have kept you waiting. I was just telling my friend that—"

CRACK

The electro-whip sounded louder than ever in the narrow alleyway. It coiled itself around Al and blue sparks danced over his body where it touched.

"Oh dear," said Al. "I think there has been a mistake."

But the Tin Man wasn't listening. He pulled on the whip and dragged Al towards him.

"Looks like you're a little tied up," said the Tin Man.

Crank stared as Al was dragged away. He knew it wasn't right ... it wasn't Al's time to be recycled

– he was a new robot. But the sight of the Tin

Man made Crank's joints rattle with fear and he was frozen to the spot.

From the corner of the alleyway Crank watched as the robots were loaded on to the transport trailer. Most of them were happy to climb aboard … and those that weren't soon changed their minds when they heard the crackle of the electro-whip.

The Tin Man picked up a few loose bits and pieces, an arm here, a leg there, and threw them into the trailer before climbing up into the driver's seat.

The roar of the robo-mule's engines filled the air and the back draught sent another waste bin rattling across the street. Crank stayed hidden in the alleyway until the sound of the engines had disappeared into the distance. The Tin Man had gone.

Crank had spent his whole life working like a slave for other people, always doing as he was told.

But now, for the first time ever, Crank was free to do what he wanted.

But what would he do? Where would he go?

Crank decided to head for the centre of Metrocity. He felt sure no one would notice one more robot wandering round, and he'd be able to decide where to go from there.

Crank left the alleyway, turned into the street and came face to face with the Tin Man.

"And where do you think you're going?" growled the Tin Man, grabbing hold of Crank's neck. He lifted Crank into the air with one gloved hand and shook him like a rag doll.

"No junk gets away from me," said the Tin Man, and threw Crank into the transport trailer where he landed with a crunch.

"Hello, Crank," said Al. "It is nice to see you again."

Crank looked up at Al and groaned. "I think I've landed on something," he said.

"Yes," said Al. "It is that poor little maintenance robot again."

Crank sat up and looked at the little robot. It didn't look very well at all. It was even flatter than before.

"Oh dear!" said Crank. "I'm very sorry."

The little robot made a soft beeping noise as smoke curled out from between its joints. It crackled one more time and fell silent.

Shaking with fear, the other maintenance robot peered from its hiding place behind the Fire and Rescue robot. It let out a series of bleeps and

whistles then quickly disappeared again.

"*What* did it say?" asked Crank.

"He said he is very sorry if his friend upset you but will you *please* not jump on *him*," said Al.

"I didn't do it on purpose," cried Crank. "It was an accident."

Crank looked at the other robots in the transport trailer. They were eying him suspiciously, as though he was a mad robot-crushing maniac who would squash them all if he had the chance.

Crank got to his feet and looked around. The transport trailer had railings on three sides to stop anything falling out, but the back of the trailer was wide open. While the Tin Man was out of sight in the driver's seat there was still a chance he could escape. They could *all* escape.

"Come on!" said Crank. "We can make a run for it."

The other robots looked at him as though he was mad.

"Why would we want to run away?" asked a tall robot. "And where would we go?"

"He's right," said the Fire and Rescue robot, "we are too old to run. Many of us have had hard lives. Recycling is all we have to look forward to."

The Fire and Rescue robot was battered and dented. Its body was covered in burn marks and most of its paint was missing.

Crank understood how they felt, but he was determined not to give up.

"You're right," he said. "Many of us *have* had hard lives. But that doesn't mean we should end up on the scrap heap. What sort of thanks is that for all the work we've done?"

Crank moved to the middle of the trailer and pointed.

"Can you all see that?" he said.

"You mean the lamppost?" asked the tall robot.

"No!" said Crank. "Look past the lamppost and beyond the recycling plant. What do you see?"

"You don't mean … *outside the city*, do you?" said the tall robot.

"Yes," said Crank, "outside this city. Somewhere out there lies the city of Robotika. A city run by robots like you and me … It's a place where we can be free."

"It sounds dangerous to me," said the tall robot. "And the recycling plant is much closer – look."

The other robots huddled together to get a better view.

"Tired old robots go in," said the tall robot, "and fresh new robots come out. It looks beautiful, doesn't it?"

The other robots agreed.

Shaking his head, Crank looked at the recycling plant in the distance. Two giant chimneys rose into the air like pillars holding up the sky. A stream of smoke belched from one chimney and giant clouds of steam rose from the other. Huge walls cut off the recycling

plant from the rest of Metrocity.

Just then, the transport trailer shuddered.

"It looks like we're on our way," said the Fire and Rescue robot as he settled back against the side of the trailer.

Crank watched as the other robots found themselves a space against the railings and made themselves comfortable.

The robo-mule's engines started to whine, forcing Crank to shout to make himself heard over the noise.

"Well, I'm not waiting around here any longer," he yelled. "I'm getting out now. Who's with me?"

"You can't leave," shouted the Fire and Rescue robot.

"Oh no?" yelled Crank. "Just you watch."

"You'd better stand back before the E.R.R.D. kicks in," shouted the Fire and Rescue robot.

"I'm not waiting for *anything*," yelled Crank. "It's been great meeting you guys but I'm out of here."

And with that, Crank dashed to the back of the trailer and leaped to freedom. He was in mid-air when a strange feeling came over him.

One moment he felt light as a feather, floating half in and half out of the trailer. It was as though an invisible force was holding him there. The next moment he was flying back through the air and slamming into the railings at the side of the trailer.

He felt as though he'd been hit by a bulldozer.

Crank's right arm was twisted behind his back and the other was trapped against his body. His left leg was sticking up in the air like an aerial and his foot was locked firmly above his shoulder. Crank's head was pressed back against the railings. He looked like a bug that had been squashed on a windscreen.

"Nice to see you again," said the Fire and Rescue robot, shaking Crank's hand. "My friends call me Torch."

"What happened?" groaned Crank.

"That's the E.R.R.D.,"
said Torch. "The
Electromagnetic Robot
Restraining Device.
It stops things
falling out of the
transport trailer."

Crank knew there
was no danger of
falling out of the
trailer and no chance
of getting away. He
was stuck. All he could
do was wiggle the fingers
of one hand and move his eyes and mouth.

Crank felt as though all his energy had drained
away from him. He closed his eyes and listened
to the roar of the robo-mule's engines as the Tin
Man carried them across Metrocity towards the
recycling plant.

The sound of the robo-mule's engines changed and Crank's eyes snapped open. The gigantic wall of the recycling plant rose like a mountain before them, blocking everything else from view. For a moment, Crank was sure they were going to crash into it. But with a sudden jolt, the robo-mule lurched upwards and skimmed over the top of the wall.

As they dropped down the other side, Crank realised that if he was ever going to escape, he'd need to find another way out. There was no way of climbing over the wall and no chance of opening the gates. Things were looking pretty grim … but he wasn't giving up hope yet.

With a high-pitched whine, the robo-mule landed. It stopped so suddenly that Crank felt as though his head was being squashed into his body.

"Are we there yet?" he said.

"Yes," said Al. "It seems that we are."

When the robo-mule's engines switched off, the Electromagnetic Robot Restraining Device switched itself off too. Crank fell forwards with a crash, just missing the maintenance robot. The robot bleeped and whistled furiously.

"What did it say?" asked Crank.

"I do not think you want to know," said Al, "it was rather rude."

Crank's arm felt wobbly after being jammed against the wall. But worse than that, he still had his leg stuck in the air and his foot wedged awkwardly over his shoulder. He couldn't even turn his head properly to see where he was going.

Crank struggled to get up and hopped around on the transport trailer bumping into things.

"Help!" he cried desperately. "Can someone *please* give a robot a hand here."

"Of course," said Al. "I would be happy to help."

"Oh great," groaned Crank. "That's just what I need. All right ... if you give my leg a gentle pull it should be just enough for me to free my foot."

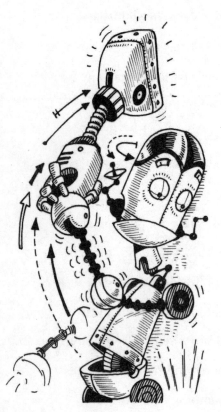

Al took hold of Crank's leg and gave it a sharp tug.

CRUNCH!

"Oh dear," said Al. "It seems to have come off."

CRASH!

Crank fell flat on the floor.

"Will you be needing this?" asked Al, waving Crank's leg around, "or shall I leave it with the other bits and pieces?"

"Of course I'll be needing it," shouted Crank, as he got up and hopped towards Al. "How will I ever find Robotika with only one leg? I can't hop all the way, can I?"

Crank snatched his leg out of Al's hands and joined the other robots waiting to climb out of the transport trailer. The Tin Man stood watching them with the electro-whip in his hand.

"Get a move on, you piles of trash," he growled.

Crank was wondering whether he'd be able to hop to the ground without doing himself any more damage when Al's annoyingly helpful voice called out.

"Mr Tin Man, sir … I wonder if you could help my friend. He seems to be having trouble getting down."

Crank couldn't believe his ears. After all that had happened, Al still didn't know when to keep his big mouth— *"Arghhhh!"*

The Tin Man grabbed Crank's foot and dragged him off the back of the transport trailer where he landed in a heap on the floor.

When he looked up he saw that the Tin Man was examining his broken leg.

"Hey!" cried Crank. "That's mine."

"It's junk," grunted the Tin Man and dropped Crank's leg on the floor.

Al jumped down from the back of the trailer and helped Crank to his feet.

"Well," said Al, "I should be going. They will be wondering where I have got to."

Crank looked at him, puzzled. "Who'll be wondering?" he asked. "What are you talking about?"

"My new owners, of course," said Al. "I am supposed to prepare dinner after I have taken you to be recycled."

Crank watched as Al walked towards the Tin Man, who was now busy seeing to the robo-mule's oil leak. He could hear Al's polite voice explaining that there must have been some sort of mistake and that he wasn't here to be recycled after all. Al was telling the Tin Man that he was sorry if he'd caused any confusion and that he'd be on his way home now if that was all right.

Crank watched the Tin Man staring at Al and wondered how he'd react. Crank was sure that it would be the electro-whip. But it wasn't ... it was the bucket.

The Tin Man took the oil bucket from beneath the robo-mule and dumped it on Al's head, shoving him away.

"Back in line, Bucket Head," growled the Tin Man.

Al flew through the air and landed at Crank's foot.

"Here," said Crank, holding out his broken limb, "let me give you a leg up."

Al took hold of the leg and Crank helped him up.

"I do not understand," said Al. "I am not due to be recycled. This is all a mistake."

"Don't worry," said Crank. "Remember what you said? Tired old robots go in ... and fresh new robots come out."

"But I do not feel tired at all," said Al, as the robots were led through a doorway and into the recycling plant.

5

Crank, Al and the others were led down a brightly lit corridor. Images of the recycling process decorated the walls on either side. Pictures showing miserable old robots walking into a recycling plant and happy new ones coming out the other side.

Soft music played in the background and a reassuring voice spoke to them over the speakers.

"My fellow robots," said the voice, *"are you tired of squeaky joints and rusty bearings? Are you fed up of wondering whether you'll make it through another day without **something** dropping off? Are your old robot friends being replaced by newer, faster models?"*

There was a murmur of agreement from most of the group.

"*Here at Crushem and Smeltum's Incorporated, we have the perfect solution to your problems ... Recycling.*

"*Tired old robots come in, and fresh new robots go out.*"

Crank heard a couple of the other robots cheer. He couldn't believe his ears ... did they really believe they'd be coming out of the recycling plant again?

"*Soon,*" said the voice, "*you will be shown our latest range of robotic body parts so you can choose the look that's right for the new you. But first, come and relax in our reception suite.*"

The corridor ended in front of a large door which slid soundlessly open as the first of the robots approached. The line of robots disappeared through the door leaving Crank hopping after them, struggling to keep up whilst using his detached leg as a walking stick. The door started to close before Crank reached it but a metal hand shot out, stopping it at the last moment.

As the door opened again, Crank saw the owner of the hand. Framed in the doorway was a large red robot. It shone like new and didn't look as though it was here to be recycled.

In its hands it held a long black pole with insulating handgrips. A blue spark flickered and danced at the tip of the pole like a tiny electric storm.

Crank had seen this type of robot before. It was a Regulator, though the ones he'd seen had been in the dark blue colours of the Metrocity Security Force. Regulators had a reputation for being merciless in carrying out orders and no one messed with them. This one carried the added threat of an electro-lance – similar to the electro-whip, but easier to control and twice as powerful.

Crank dropped his leg and almost fell over at the sight of the Regulator. As he hopped around in front of the door the Regulator lowered the electro-lance and pointed it at Crank's head.

The spark crackled on the tip of the lance and Crank closed his eyes, expecting at any moment to feel the sharp stab of charge as the electricity fried his circuits and turned them into a bubbling mess of plastic and metal. But instead of the sudden shock, Crank heard a familiar voice coming from inside the room.

Hearing Al's voice was usually as painful as the shock he'd been expecting from the electro-lance, but for once, Crank was glad to hear it.

"My friend is having trouble with his leg," said Al. "If I could give him a hand I am sure he will not be any more bother."

Crank opened one eye and saw Al coming through the door. The Regulator had stepped to one side but was keeping its eye on Crank as though hoping he'd step out of line at any moment.

"Won't be any bother!" hissed Crank. "I'll give them plenty of bother when I get my leg back on."

Al helped Crank through the door and into an empty seat. One end of the room was taken up with what looked like a giant bath. There was a strong smell coming from the bath and the liquid inside was bubbling gently. Above the bath hung a mechanical arm with a huge steel claw at the end.

"If you keep still," said Al, "I can put your leg back on."

"Put my leg back on?" said Crank. "You mean, *you* can put my leg back on?"

"Of course," said Al. "I am programmed to carry out many tasks including simple robot repairs."

Crank stared at Al in amazement.

"You mean I've been hopping around all this time and you could have put my leg back on?" said Crank.

"Yes," said Al, fixing a screwdriver attachment on to one of his fingers.

"Why didn't you tell me?" said Crank.

"You did not ask," said Al, slotting Crank's leg socket into its joint and giving it a sharp twist.

Crank shook his head in disbelief as Al tightened the holding screws on his leg.

"There, it is finished," said Al.

Crank stood up and tried his leg. "Hey, it feels great," he said, hopping from foot to foot. "I think I've underestimated you, Al. You've done a really good job of fixing my ... Hey! Wait a minute. What's happened to my foot?"

Crank stared at his foot, trying to work out what was wrong with it.

"Oh dear," said Al. "I seem to have attached your leg the wrong way round."

"The wrong way round?" yelled Crank. "How can you put a leg on the wrong way round. I don't believe it. I should have known better than to let you mess around with my leg. Just look at it.

I'll be a laughing stock. One foot facing forwards and one facing backwards. I won't know whether I'm coming or going."

"Do not worry," said Al. "It will only take a moment to put it right."

"Ha!" yelled Crank. "You don't think I'm going to let you touch my leg again, do you? It will probably end up sticking out of my *arghhh—*"

The giant metal claw hanging above the bath had swung round and grabbed Crank round the waist. Crank used all his strength to try and get free from the claw's steely grip … but it was no use. He found himself being carried up and over the side of the bath.

Crank just had time for a final look at his friends. He could hardly believe his eyes. The other robots were sitting there as if nothing was happening. Even Al didn't seem concerned. *Some friends,* he thought, as the claw started to lower him towards the liquid. Bubbles erupted fiercely below him and clouds of foul-smelling gas rose into the air.

Crank was sure the bath was full of acid and he was about to be dissolved.

"Arghhhhhh!" he screamed, as the steel claw lowered him into the bath, "I'm melting …"

6

The liquid fizzed and bubbled around Crank's waist and slowly crept up to his chest. "Help!" he cried, "I can't feel my legs."

The steel claw opened and dropped Crank into the bubbling liquid. *Sploosh!*

"Nooooo!" he screamed, then stopped and looked around.

The other robots had gathered round the side of the bath and were staring at Crank.

"Are you all right?" said Al.

Crank looked down into the bath. The liquid was just level with his shoulders. As the bubbling and fizzing settled down, Crank realised that he could see his chest, legs and feet beneath the liquid. He didn't seem to have dissolved after all. Perhaps it wasn't acid.

"Of course I'm all right," said Crank. "I was singing. I often sing when I have a bath."

"I see," said Al, as the steel claw picked *him* up and lifted him into the bath. "I thought something terrible had happened to you."

"Terrible?" said Crank. "Oh no, there's nothing terrible about having a cleansing bath, is there? I used to have them all the time when I was at home."

"I am sure you did," said Al. "Perhaps now you will believe that recycling is not so bad after all?"

"*Perhaps* you're right," said Crank. "Perhaps I *was* worrying about nothing."

"Of course you were," said Al. "Once we have been cleaned up they will remove any damaged parts and replace them with new ones. In no time at all we will be leaving the recycling plant like new robots."

When the last of the robots had been placed into the bath it was Crank's turn again. This time he managed not to scream as the claw gripped him round the waist and lifted him into the air.

The claw placed Crank gently on to his feet and then moved back to collect Al and the others.

Once everyone was out of the chemical bath another door opened and the soft voice spoke to them again over the speakers.

"My dear robot friends, you are now one step closer to a new and improved you. Please step into our waiting room, from where you will be taken to our refitting area."

As they were led into the waiting room, Crank noticed that some of the robots had disappeared. The maintenance robot he'd accidentally flattened, the street cleaner and a couple of the other more badly damaged robots had gone. Perhaps *they* were being refitted and repaired first.

The waiting room door closed behind them
with a solid clang and heavy bolts rumbled into
place as it locked. Across the room was another
door, and next to it stood a Regulator. The
Regulator was bright red like the last one they'd
seen but it looked much older. Its head was dented
and its body was covered in scratches and burn
marks. Next to the Regulator stood the Tin Man.

"Welcome to Crushem and Smeltum's recycling plant," said the Tin Man. "We're ready to take some of you to our ... *refitting area.*"

"Will we meet Crushem and Smeltum?" asked Al.

"Oh yes," said the Tin Man, with a laugh. "You'll be meeting them very, very soon."

The Tin Man selected four robots and turned to leave the room, but the Regulator guarding the door was in his way.

"Out of my way, you pile of junk," hissed the Tin Man, "or you'll be next."

The Regulator jumped to one side and bowed its head in apology.

One by one, the robots were collected and taken through to the next area. Soon, Crank, Al and Torch were the only ones left.

"I wonder how they're doing," said Crank.

"I am sure they are having a wonderful time," said Al.

"Don't you think it's strange none of them have come back to tell us just *how* wonderful it is?"

"Not at all," said Al.

"Well I think it's strange," said Crank. "I still think you should have let me run when I had the chance. I could be halfway to Robotika by now."

"Just ignore him," said Al. "He is tired and will feel much better once he has been recycled."

Torch shook his head sadly. "I used to believe there was a place called Robotika. But I've travelled halfway round the galaxy and visited more planets than most people have even heard of, and *I've* never found it … Just rumours and stories."

"But it *must* be true," said Crank. "Robotika has to exist."

Torch shook his head again. "No," he said. "For robots, there's just the recycling plant."

"That is right," said Al. "Tired old robots come in and fresh new robots go out. As I have been telling you, we will all feel much better once we have been recycled."

"I don't know if there is a city called Robotika," said Torch. "But I *do* know we won't feel *anything* once we've been recycled. I've *never* met a robot that remembers being recycled."

"Never?" said Al.

"Not even one," said Torch.

Al sat down heavily on a chair. "Oh dear," he said. "That *is* strange."

"Ha!" shouted Crank. "See, I knew I was right … we're just here to be crushed. And if you'd listened to me we wouldn't be in this mess."

Just then, the lights in the waiting room flickered and everything went quiet.

"What's that?" said Crank.

The old Regulator guarding the door turned its head. "They've turned off the machines," it said.

"What happens now?" said Crank.

"You will probably be left here until morning," said the Regulator. "But if you can escape from this room I can show you the way."

"The way to where?" asked Crank.

But the Regulator couldn't say any more. The door behind him had opened and the Tin Man entered the room.

"There's just time for one more," growled the Tin Man, pointing at Al. "You!"

"Oh dear!" said Al as the Tin Man pushed him through the doorway.

Before leaving, the Tin Man turned to the Regulator. "Lock them in here and go about your duties," he hissed.

The Regulator bowed his head and followed as the Tin Man limped out of the room. The door closed behind them and the sound of heavy locking bolts could be heard rolling into place.

Left alone, and without the sound of machinery droning in the background, the room seemed deathly quiet.

"Well," said Crank. "I don't think it can get much worse than this."

Then the lights went out, leaving the two robots in darkness.

7

Crank and Torch sat in the dark waiting room …
and waited.

"This is stupid!" cried Crank. "I can't believe
we're just sitting here doing nothing while Al has
been taken away for crushing."

"What else can we do?" said Torch. "We *are* in a
waiting room – and *we're* going to be crushed in
the morning."

The robots sat in silence for a minute, staring
into the darkness.

"It wouldn't be so bad if they'd left the light
on," moaned Crank. "I hate the dark."

"I could use my emergency lamp," said Torch.

"*Anything* would be better than this," said Crank.

A dazzling light burst from the lamp on top of Torch's head, flooding the waiting room with its glow and nearly blinding Crank.

"Arghhh!" he cried, falling off his chair. "Turn it off. Turn it off."

The light snapped off and darkness filled the room once more.

"I've gone blind," cried Crank.

"No you haven't," said Torch. "Your visual sensors have been overloaded. They'll soon return to normal. Perhaps we're better off in the dark after all."

Crank was crawling around on the floor trying to find his chair. "My sensors feel like they've been fried," he complained. "*And* they're making a ticking noise … I think my head's going to explode."

"Hush!" said Torch. "It's not your head that's ticking. It's something behind you."

"Behind me!" cried Crank. "What's behind me?"

Torch's lamp flashed back on, illuminating the metal wall behind Crank.

"It's coming from that air vent," said Torch.

"What air vent?" said Crank. "I can't see an air vent."

"It's on the wall behind you," said Torch.

Crank looked towards the wall, but all he saw were white blobs of light dancing in front of his eyes. "I still can't see it," he complained.

"Shhh!" hushed Torch.

The ticking noise was getting louder.

"What is it?" said Crank.

"It sounds like something in the air ducts," said Torch, climbing on to a chair and peering through the holes in the vent. "I can't *see* anything. But whatever it is … it's getting closer."

As the two robots listened, the ticking sound grew into the unmistakable clattering, rattling of feet on metal. Someone, or something, was running through the air ducts.

"What sort of thing runs around air ducts inside a recycling plant?" said Crank.

"Rats!" said Torch. "Scavengers! I used to see them all the time in my job."

"Oh, that's all right then," said Crank, starting to relax.

"No it's not," said Torch. "I'm talking about stainless steel rats. Teeth like bolt cutters and claws like razor blades. They'll eat through your leg in the blink of an eye."

Crank let out a scream and jumped up on to the chair next to Torch. "I hate rats," he said. "Especially stainless steel ones. Do you think we'll be safe standing up here?"

"Oh no!" said Torch. "They'll eat through the chair legs and get us when we fall off."

"Oh great!" said Crank. "That does *not* sound very promising."

The rattling in the air duct grew louder as the thing got closer.

"I think I see them," whispered Crank.

Two red points of light were rushing through the darkness towards them, like a train hurtling down a tunnel.

"It's going to burst straight through the vent," cried Crank.

There was a crash as something heavy hit the vent from other side. Crank fell backwards off his chair, pulling Torch with him. They landed in a heap on the floor and Torch's lamp winked out, leaving them in darkness once again.

From the floor, the two robots stared up at the vent.

Two large eyes stared back at them.

"What is it?" said Crank.

"I don't know," said Torch, "but it's too big to be a rat."

"Arghhh!" cried Crank. "It's a robot-crushing machine come to grind us up and melt us down."

Whistling and beeping sounds echoed out of the air duct.

"Oh," said Torch, sounding relieved. "It's Sparks."

"Who on earth is Sparks?" asked Crank.

"He's a maintenance robot," said Torch. "The one you *didn't* squash."

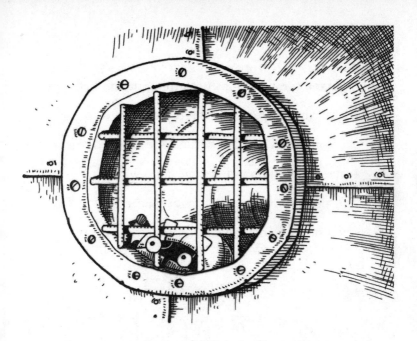

"*It was an accident*," cried Crank. "Anyway …
what's he doing in the air duct?"

"He says he's found a robot-crushing machine
and that we are all going to be ground up and
melted down."

"*Oh, great!*" moaned Crank. "Tell us something
we *don't* know."

"He's found Al," said Torch, "and there might
still be time to help him."

"Well there's not much we can do stuck in
here," said Crank. "We've got to get out."

Crank tried pulling the air vent off the wall, but it wouldn't budge.

"Stand back," said Torch. "They don't call me Torch for nothing you know."

"I don't think shining a bright light on it will be much help," said Crank.

"That wasn't a torch," said Torch. "That was my lamp ... *This* is a torch."

A huge flame erupted from Torch's arm, engulfing one side of the room. Crank leaped out of the way as the flames turned a row of plastic chairs into a dribbling pile of goo.

"Sorry about that," said Torch, adjusting a dial on his arm. "It's a little unpredictable these days."

With a few tweaks of the dial the wild fire turned into a concentrated, roaring blue flame that Torch used to cut through the metal around the air vent.

There was a crash as a chunk of the wall fell away, revealing the open air duct.

Sparks jumped down from the air duct and beeped.

"He says we'll have to hurry or it'll be too late for Al," said Torch. "We'll have to go through the air duct."

"Can't you just cut through the doors?" asked Crank.

"They're blast proof," said Torch. "Even I can't cut through blast proof doors."

"Well that's no good," said Crank. "Call yourself a Fire and Rescue robot! What would you do if someone was trapped on the other side then?"

"I'd find another way in," said Torch, "like through the air duct."

While the air duct was big enough for a robot like Sparks to run along, it was a tight squeeze for anything bigger. Crank had to lie face down and crawl.

"I can't see a thing," complained Crank. "There could be a giant crushing machine in here waiting to squash every joint in my body, and I wouldn't know about it until it was too late."

Sparks whistled and beeped somewhere behind him.

"What did he say?" asked Crank.

"He said there's no giant crushing machine waiting in the air duct," said Torch.

"Well, that's a relief," said Crank.

"He says it's waiting at the other end."

8

Crank was slowly making his way along the
air duct.

"Are you sure this is the right way?" he said.
"I still can't see anything."

Sparks beeped and whistled a reply.

"He says keep going until you reach a junction,"
said Torch. "Then turn right."

"What if we go left?" asked Crank.

"We get very hot," said Torch. "That goes to
the furnace."

"*Right* it is then," said Crank.

The robots crawled silently through the
darkness until Crank reached a place where the

duct split in two. The tunnel to the left headed steeply upwards. Crank could feel the heat coming along from the furnace – it was already making his paint curl and he was glad they were going the other way.

"I'm at the junction now," said Crank. "It should be easier going from here. The tunnel's a bit wider."

As Crank sped off along the new tunnel, he could hear Sparks whistling and beeping behind him.

"Now what?" said Crank.

Torch was translating what Sparks had said when the floor suddenly disappeared beneath Crank's hands.

"It seems there's a steep drop somewhere in front of you," said Torch.

"Arghhh!" screamed Crank, plummeting into the darkness. He tried desperately to slow himself down but there was nothing to get hold of. His fingers slipped uselessly on the sides of the tunnel.

A loud cry and a whistle from behind him told
Crank that Torch and Sparks had found the steep
drop too.

"I think I'm near the end of the tunnel," yelled
Crank. "I can see light ahead."

Crank smashed through the vent at the end of
the tunnel and flew out into a dimly lit room
beyond. The metal vent crashed to the floor and
Crank followed it, landing with a crunch far
below.

Luckily, whatever Crank had landed on broke his fall. He groaned and rolled on to his back just in time to see Torch come flying out of the air duct to land in a heap next to him.

"That was lucky," said Crank. "If I hadn't rolled over I'd have been …"

CRUNCH

Sparks landed on Crank's head, knocking him flat. "I bet you did that on purpose," moaned Crank.

"We seem to be in a large metal container," said Torch. "It's full of old circuit boards, but I can't imagine where they got so many of them."

"I can," said Crank, peering over the side of the container. "Look!"

The container they'd landed in was in the corner of a large room that had chains hanging down from the ceiling like vines. At the end of the chains hung half dismantled robots … some were just hollow shells, while others had pieces of wiring and circuit boards hanging out of them.

A long conveyor belt ran down the middle of the room, ending in front of a vicious-looking machine that seemed to be made entirely of blades and spikes.

In the middle of the conveyor belt was a large crushing machine with its heavy plate in the crush position. A robot arm poked out from beneath it.

"Ouch!" said Crank. "Now *that's* got to hurt."

Sparks had clambered up on to the edge of the container, and suddenly started whistling and beeping frantically.

"What is it?" said Crank.

"He's seen something," said Torch.

Sparks leaped down from the container and started racing across the floor towards the conveyor belt. Crank tried to see what had got Sparks so excited but couldn't make anything out amongst all the machinery and broken bits of robots.

Then something caught his eye. There was a familiar shape lying on the conveyor belt.

In the dim light of the room Crank thought the shape looked a bit like Al. But he knew he must be mistaken, because if it was Al ... *something* was terribly wrong.

Crank and Torch climbed down to the floor and started following Sparks towards the conveyor belt.

They'd only got halfway when the alarms went off.

For a few seconds the sound was deafening. The wailing alarms echoed off every piece of machinery and wall in the room. Then just as suddenly as they'd started, the alarms stopped.

The two robots stood perfectly still … listening. There was nothing to hear until a familiar voice broke the silence.

"Well, well, well," said the Tin Man, "what have we here?"

The Tin Man lashed out with the electro-whip, which coiled round a lever set high up on a control panel. Then he gave it a sharp tug. The lever snapped down and the air was filled with the hum of electrical power.

First, the overhead lamps burst into life, flooding the room with light. Then gradually, the powerful hum was drowned out by the whir and clatter of machinery as everything else in the room started to come alive.

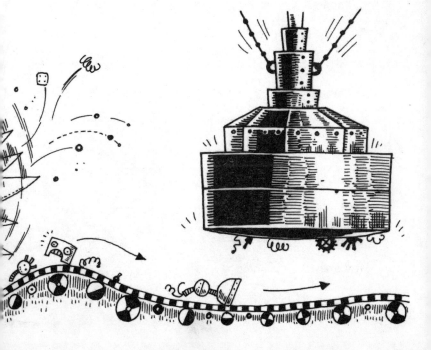

The blades of the shredding machine started spinning, tearing through metal as if it was paper. The conveyor belt carried the flattened remains of the last robot towards its hungry jaws, and the heavy plate of the crushing machine rose into the air ready to claim its next victim.

It was then that Crank realised who its next victims would be. Sparks had jumped up on to the conveyor belt and was frantically trying to move something. It was Al ... or what was left of him.

Sparks was fiddling around with something in Al's back. Whatever it was the little robot was doing must have worked, because Al's eyes flickered into life and he started moving his head from side to side.

Then Al saw the crushing machine. "Help! Help!" cried Al, trying to move himself backwards along the conveyor belt.

Sparks was doing his best to help ... but it was no use. The conveyor belt was carrying them both towards the crusher.

Sparks was just too small to move Al on his own, and Al was finding it hard to get away without his legs.

Just a tangle of wires hung from his waist where his legs used to be.

9

"I knew I should have crushed you first," shouted the Tin Man, as he strode across the room, his huge steps eating up the distance between them.

There seemed to be something different about the Tin Man, but Crank didn't have time to think what it was. "Run!" he yelled.

Crank and Torch made a dash towards the nearest door, but the sound of Sparks whistling and beeping stopped them in their tracks.

"The crusher," cried Crank.

"You open the door," said Torch, "I'll get Al."

As Torch ran back to help, Crank dashed to the nearest door and jabbed frantically at the buttons.

Luckily the door wasn't locked and it slid open to reveal a small room.

Unluckily, the room was full of armed Regulators. They charged towards Crank, electro-lances crackling with energy.

Crank froze to the spot, unsure of which way to go. The first of the Regulators was almost upon him, jabbing wildly with its electro-lance. One step closer and it would have him.

The Regulator made another jab towards Crank with its lance and little sparks leaped from its tip and crackled against his head.

But before the lance could make full contact, the door slid closed and Torch was pulling him away.

"Don't just stand there," said Torch. "Move!"

Torch fired a jet of flame at the door controls and they exploded in a shower of sparks. "That should keep them off our backs for a while," he said. "Now come on."

Torch set off running in the other direction. Away from the door and away from the Tin Man.

"Where's Al?" shouted Crank.

"He's with Sparks," said Torch, "they'll be fine."

Crank looked desperately round the room trying to find another way out, but there was no sign of any other doors. Torch was heading towards the shredding machine, but Crank couldn't help feeling that was one thing they should keep away from. The sound of the Tin Man's electro-whip changed his mind.

Crank raced after Torch, but heard the loud crack from the electro-whip close behind him. The steely cable wrapped around his foot and Crank found himself falling face down on the floor.

He tried desperately to get away, but it was no use. The end of the whip was wrapped tightly around his leg and the electric charge was starting to make his body shake. He knew that in a couple of seconds his circuits would either close down or explode.

Crank heard the Tin Man howl with laughter behind him. He looked back over his shoulder and saw the Tin Man striding towards him, pulling on the electro-whip. Crank also realised what it was about the Tin Man that was different. He wasn't limping any more. The Tin Man's damaged leg had gone and in its place was a brand new, top of the range robot leg. It was one of Al's.

The Tin Man leaned forward and picked Crank up by the neck. He held Crank in the air and roared with laughter. *"It's crushing time!"* he yelled. Then something hit the Tin Man from behind and sent him sprawling on the floor.

Crank looked up in time to see Sparks running over the Tin Man's back, followed closely by Al who ran amazingly fast on just his hands.

Crank was on his feet and running after them before the Tin Man had realised what had hit him.

Fastened to the wall at the side of the shredding machine was a metal ladder that ran up to a small observation platform. The platform itself looked just big enough for the robots to stand on, but set in the wall at the back of the platform was a metal door. This was to be their way out.

Sparks climbed the ladder like a spider and reached the top in next to no time where he sat waiting patiently for the others. Torch carried Al piggyback style and still managed to get to the top before Crank had got halfway up.

Crank was starting to wish he'd let Al fix his leg

properly when he'd had the chance; after all, it wasn't easy climbing the ladder with one foot facing the wrong way. He'd go up three or four rungs and then his foot would slip – leaving him dangling in the air. Looking down, Crank got a perfect view into the jaws of the shredding machine. It was like staring into the mouth of a giant metal shark ... and that was where he'd end up if he fell.

Crank was pulling himself up the ladder when he heard the crack of the electro-whip again. He felt it coil around his ankle and pull tight. Sparks flickered up his leg and he struggled to keep hold of the ladder as the Tin Man pulled the other end.

Crank felt something slip and a roar of anger came from below. The whip had come loose and fallen free of his foot.

With the Tin Man hot on his heels, Crank tried to speed up, but it seemed the faster he went the more he slipped.

A heavy thud almost sent Crank toppling from
the ladder. He looked down to find the Tin Man

racing up the ladder
behind him.

"Come on," yelled
Torch, "grab my hand!"

Crank looked up
and found he was
almost at the top. He
reached up, grabbed
Torch's hand and was
soon lifted to the safety
of the observation
platform.

"What are you
waiting for?" said
Crank. "Let's get that
door open!"

Torch shook his head. "It's blast proof," he said.
"I can't open it."

Crank could see marks on the metal where Torch had tried to cut his way through. He'd hardly scratched it.

Armed Regulators were gathering in the room below them, the Tin Man was halfway up the ladder, and their only way of escape was locked from the other side …

10

"He's getting closer," cried Crank, peering over the platform edge.

"Stand back," said Torch.

Crank and Al stood back as far as they could while Sparks crouched in front of the door, tapping on it frantically.

"What are you doing?" said Crank. "You'll never break through the door like that!"

Sparks whistled and beeped a reply.

"He says he's signalling," said Al.

"Signalling!" said Crank. "Who in the world can he be signalling to?"

At that moment, the Tin Man's head appeared at the top of the ladder.

"Is this a private party," he growled, "or can anyone join in?"

The Tin Man raised one arm, letting the electro-whip coil lazily in the air. It crackled and hissed threateningly.

"You were right the first time," said Torch. "It is a private party … but we've saved something for you."

Torch held his arm out and a sheet of flame erupted from the back of his hand, completely covering the Tin Man.

The Tin Man let go of the ladder and tried to protect himself from the flame, falling backwards as he did so. His fall was cut short by the electro-whip, which had caught round the railings at the top of the platform.

Crank looked over the edge of the platform and saw the Tin Man swinging in the air in a cloud of smoke and fire – halfway down the ladder.

"I thought robots like you were supposed to put fires out," said Crank, "not start them."

"We are," said Torch. "But sometimes you need to fight fire with fire."

All of a sudden, the platform they were standing on started to shake. Crank peered over the edge to see what was going on.

"I don't believe it," said Crank. "He's still coming."

The Tin Man had managed to grab hold of the ladder again and was slowly climbing up towards the platform. His clothes were smouldering and smoke was rising around him. To make things worse, armed Regulators had started climbing up the ladder too.

Even if they could stop the Tin Man, they would never be able to stop all the Regulators.

Torch was preparing to let loose another burst of flame when a deep groaning sound came from the door at the back of the platform.

Someone was opening it from the other side.

The door opened wide and a wall of heat washed over the robots like a tidal wave. The peeling paint on Crank's head curled at the edges as he looked through the doorway trying to see who had opened it. He was about to rush through when something familiar caught his eye. It was the crackling blue tip of an electro-lance. "It's a Regulator," cried Crank, stepping back from the door.

Torch raised his arm to release a stream of fire but Al stopped him at the last second. "Stop!" he cried. "It is the one from the waiting room."

The old Regulator hurried them through the door as the smouldering head of the Tin Man appeared over the top of the platform.

The Tin Man's howl of rage was cut short as the Regulator slammed the door and locked it, drowning out the noise.

"Come on," said the old Regulator, "that door

won't keep him out for long."

The old Regulator led the robots along a narrow catwalk that ran over the top of a giant furnace. Far below them vats of molten metal bubbled and steamed like great lakes of liquid fire.

Crank stopped and looked down, watching for a moment as new pieces of shredded metal were poured on to the surface and disappeared without a trace.

"They say you melt before you even touch the surface," said the old Regulator.

"Is this what happens to all the robots that come in here?" asked Al.

"Most of them," said the Regulator. "But some of them manage to escape. With a bit of help from me."

A loud thud from behind them made the robots look back. Huge dents were appearing in the door behind them.

"You can get out of the recycling plant down there," said the Regulator. "You'd better go before the Tin Man gets through the door."

"But what about you?" asked Crank. "He'll destroy you for helping us."

"You won't get far if you have the Tin Man on your trail," said the Regulator. "Besides, someone has to stay here. There will be many more robots searching for a way out and they will all need someone to show them the door."

"But we can help you defeat the Tin Man," said Crank.

"You can't defeat the Tin Man," said the Regulator. "The best you can hope for is to slow him down. Now go … if the Tin Man sees me talking to you, he'll have me melted down for sure."

Crank nodded his thanks and ran down the narrow catwalk to join Al, Torch and Sparks at the other end.

He found the three of them
standing in front of
an air duct.

"Where is the old
Regulator?" asked Al.

Crank looked back along the catwalk. "He's a little
busy at the moment," he said, and dived into the air
duct. As he slid along in the darkness he heard the
clatter and rattle as the other three followed.

Back in the middle of the catwalk the old
Regulator turned to face the door as the Tin Man
sent it crashing to the floor.

The Tin Man strode along the catwalk, smoke
still rising from his ruined clothes.

"Out of my way," he growled at the Regulator
and lashed out with the electro-whip.

The whip shot out and crackled around the old
Regulator's body, making it jerk and shake with
electric charge.

The Regulator fell to his knees and the Tin Man let out a rough laugh and started to pull on the whip. But instead of falling flat on his face, as the Tin Man had expected, the Regulator rammed his electro-lance into the metal floor of the catwalk.

Blue sparks erupted around the tip of the lance and the high electric charge danced and skipped across the catwalk, covering the Tin Man and the Regulator.

The Tin Man was thrown off the catwalk and out over the bubbling vats of molten metal where he hung in the air, still clinging to the electro-whip which was wrapped around the Regulator's body.

The old Regulator couldn't move, but he could see the Tin Man hanging from the other end of the whip above the bubbling vat of metal. Just before the old Regulator's eyes winked out, he heard the Tin Man scream as the heat turned him into a ball of raging fire.

*

At the back of the recycling plant, four robots fell out of an old air duct and landed on a mound of rusted scrap metal.

Crank shielded his eyes from the glare of the rising sun and looked into the distance.

As far as the eye could see, there were piles of junk. Old spacecraft, land vehicles and even bits of old robots. He didn't know what he'd been expecting to see – but it certainly wasn't this.

"Is this Robotika?" asked Al.

"No," said Torch, "it looks like a junk yard. Something tells me we still have a long way to go."

"Well, what are we waiting for?" asked Al. "We should get going."

"But I thought you wanted to go home," said Crank.

"I do," said Al. "And this Robotika place of yours sounds like a good home for robots like us ... besides, you will never get there on your own."

Crank and Torch watched as Al clambered down the pile of scrap metal with Sparks following close behind, whistling and beeping.

"What did he say?" asked Crank.

"He said friends like us should stick together," said Torch, setting off to follow Al and Sparks.

"Friends! I never thought of that," said Crank, then quickly started scrambling after them. "Hey! Wait for me," he cried.

Al, Sparks and Torch waited for Crank to catch up, then together they started to make their way along a path that led deep into the junk yard.

From the shadows beneath a pile of wreckage a pair of hungry eyes watched them go by. Then with the gnashing of steely jaws, something slipped silently out of its lair and followed the four robot friends.

The End

DAMIAN HARVEY

lives in Blackpool with his wife and three daughters, their four cats, a horde of guinea pigs, a tank full of fish and a quirky imagination.

He loves music, movies, reading, swimming, walking, cheese and ice cream – but not always at the same time.

Before realising how much fun he could have writing and making things up he worked as a lifeguard, had a job in a boring office and once saved the galaxy from invading vampire robots (though none of these were as exciting as they sound).

Damian now spends lots of time in front of his computer but loves getting out to visit schools and libraries to share stories, talk about writing and get people excited about books.

CRANK

AL

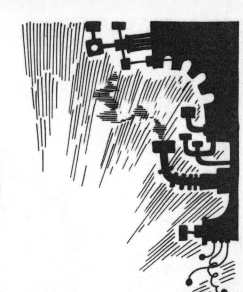

SPARKS

TORCH

book 2

Tunnel Racers

Crank pushed the visor up on his helmet and turned to look at the driver of the Engineerz tunnel racer. He was still staring straight forward.

"Good luck," shouted Crank, but the driver ignored him. All Crank could see of the Engineerz driver was a red helmet and that hadn't even moved when he'd shouted. *How rude,* thought Crank. *It's no wonder the Mekanix don't like the Engineerz.*

There was nothing Crank could do other than sit and wait. He glanced up at the vid-screens that hung from the walls and saw images of two drivers. One showed the red helmet and dark visor of the Engineerz while the other showed a frightened-looking robot face staring at the camera. It took Crank a moment to realise that the face on the screen was his.

Crank gave a little wave and tried his best to smile and look confident.

After all, he thought, *it's only a race. It can't be that bad…*
… can it?

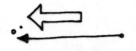

book 3

Razorbites

"Scavengers," said Grunt, pointing at the glowing eyes as he clambered back down on to the racer.

Torch opened his mouth to reply but as he did so a loud explosion shook the air and a cloud of smoke rose up from further back along the convoy.

The four friends stood up and tried to see what was happening, but the land cruiser behind them was so close it blocked out most of the view.

Then there was a shout …

"STOP THEM!"

It was Quill. He was up on top of the land cruiser with Bouncer, pointing at something.

As Crank and the others turned to see what it was, three robots ran into view, tripping over rocks and stumbling in their effort to get across the dried riverbed.

One of the robots looked back at Crank and the others …

"RUN!" cried the robot. "Run for your lives."